This edition published in the UK by Scholastic, 2022
1 London Bridge, London, SE1 9BA
Scholastic Ireland, 89E Lagan Road, Dublin Industrial
Estate, Glasnevin, Dublin, D11 HP5F

First published in the UK by Scholastic, 2018

Text and illustrations © Matt Carr, 2018

ISBN 978 07023 2271 6

A CIP catalogue record for this book is available
from the British Library.

Printed in China
Paper made from wood grown in sustainable forests
and other controlled sources.

10 9 8 7 6 5 4 3 2 1

www.scholastic.co.uk

Some names have been changed to conceal the identities
of secret agents involved in this book.

For Delilah, Coco,
Edie, Connie, Alice
& Hattie! M.C.

DER

MATT CARR

SCHOLASTIC

It was a special day at Number 7 Fleming Road.
Little Tom Webster's birthday was about to start
and everyone was excited...

...especially Spyder, the world's smallest secret agent
who lived in the loft. She loved birthdays.

In her penthouse flat
Spyder had just put her feet up
(which takes quite a while when you've got eight legs).

Suddenly her spy phone rang...

RING!
RING!

It was **Headquarters**, with an urgent message.

Spyder leapt into action.

Hello, 008.
This naughty fellow has just entered your airspace.
If he reaches the kitchen, Tom's precious birthday cake could be ruined.

On my way, Boss. You know I never like to miss a party!

CODE NAME: BLUEBOTTLE

SEE-THROUGH WINGS

VERY CHEEKY ATTITUDE

BIG BULGY EYES

6 HAIRY LEGS

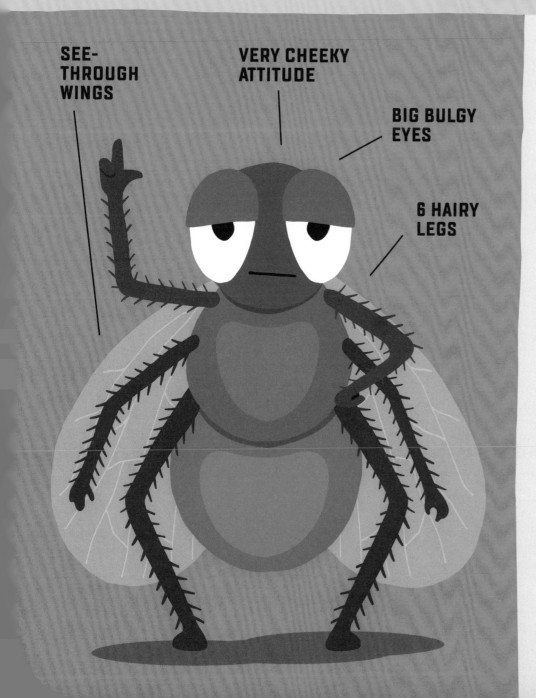

FACT FILE:

- LOVES SWEET TREATS, ESPECIALLY CAKE!

- ALSO LIKES EATING RUBBISH AND OTHER STINKY STUFF. URGH!

- CARRIES QUITE A FEW GERMS AROUND WHICH YOU WOULDN'T WANT ON A BIRTHDAY CAKE. YUCK!

- DEFINITELY **NOT** INVITED TO THE PARTY!

Binoculars

Banana

Spy camera

Top-secret laser pen

Disguise

Flask of tea

THE DAILY WEB

TINY SPIDER WINS LOTTERY!

"I'M REALLY LUCKY" SAYS MONEY SPIDER

Newspaper

Spyder quickly packed her spy-kit, and set off.

Just getting around the house was a near-impossible mission, but that didn't bother Spyder.

DANGER* was her middle name!

*Actually, it's Dorothy!

Soon, she came face to face
with her first obstacle:
a huge, strange, hairy creature
with terrible breath.

It's too **BIG** to be a fly!
she thought.

Stop right there, Mr Bottle!

No can do, Spyder, I've got a date with a cake!

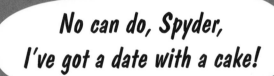

Bluebottle was heading for the bathroom.

Spyder gave chase...

but she didn't notice a thudding sound that was getting louder...

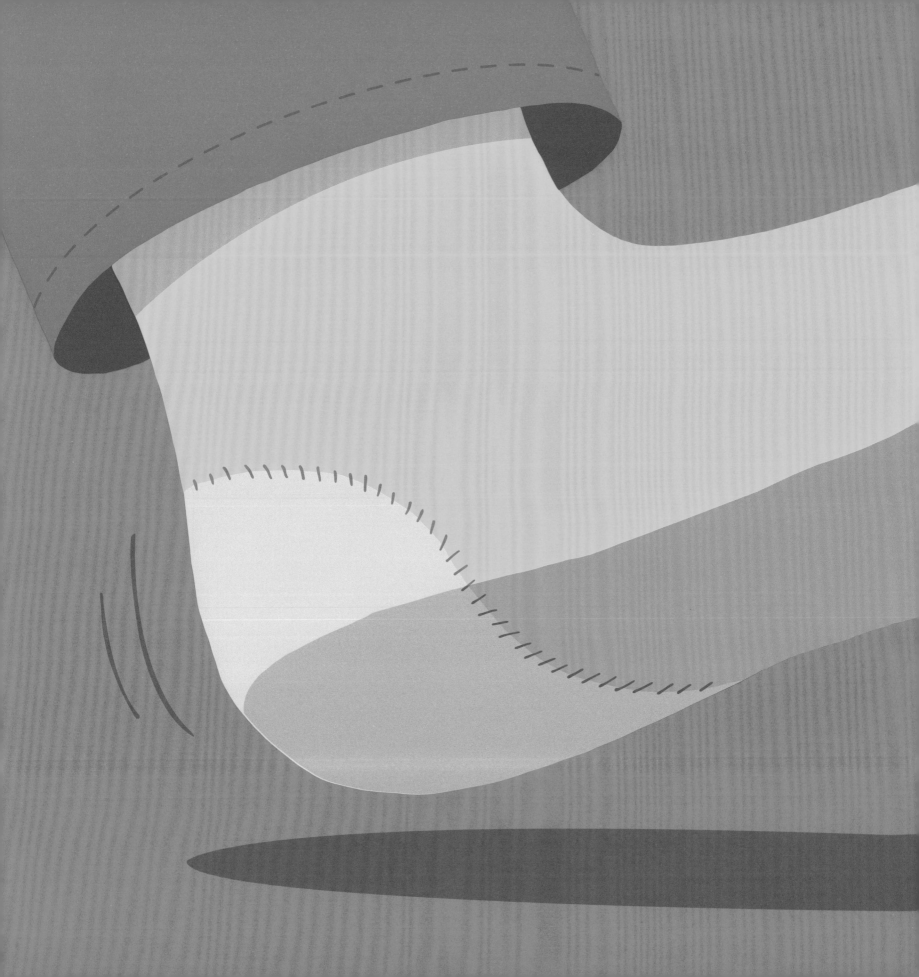

Spyder swung down...

but could
not see the
pesky pest
anywhere.
Until...

Bluebottle
zoomed
down...

and knocked poor
Spyder into the bath.

OUCH!

Spyder landed on her bottom with a THUMP!
Bluebottle chuckled. He knew baths were the one place
spiders had trouble getting out of.

Just then Spyder's phone beeped again.

She looked around the tub for an escape route...

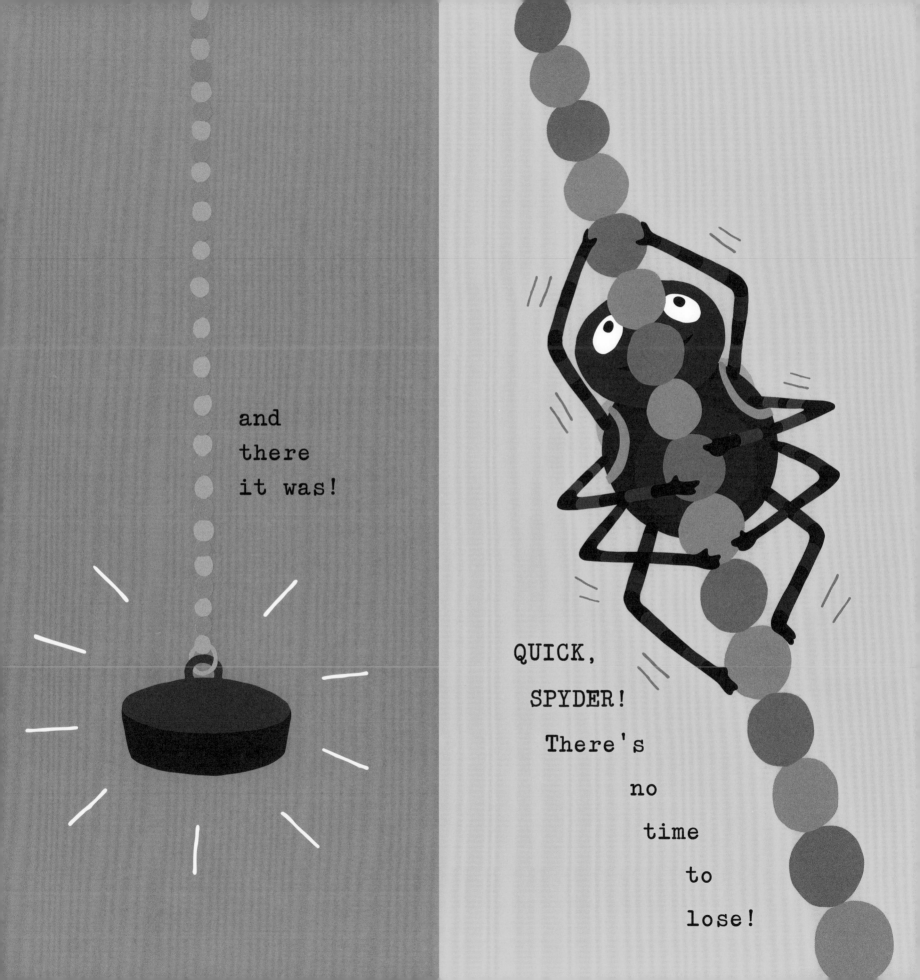

In the kitchen,
Bluebottle was
circling hungrily.

Sugar

TASTY LEMONADE

Spyder would have to think on her feet
(lucky she had lots of them!).

Tom's cake looked splendid.
Bluebottle was sure to
spot it soon.

Spyder threw out a fine silk line....

...and bravely climbed across.

She spun a super strong web...

and then she waited...

Bluebottle spied the cake
and dived down at top speed...

straight into Spyder's sticky web!

Spyder had saved the day – and the cake!

Sorry, my friend – the party's over!

You win, Spyder! I suppose I'd better buzz off!

Well done, Spyder! I'm sure the Websters will be very happy!

She cleared away her web and soon the cake was as good as new.

MISSION ACCOMPLISHED!

RING! RING!

MISS MONEY SPIDER

AAAA
A

SPIDER FACTS WEBSITE!

STRONG!

A spider's web may look thin and flimsy, but it is in fact very STRONG.

A spider's silk is even stronger than steel!

SCARY!

The fear of spiders is called... ARACHNOPHOBIA but spiders are actually a lot more scared of humans!

SPEEDY!

Some spiders are VERY fast indeed and could run even faster than a car if they were the same size as us!

SUPER-SIZE!

Spiders come in all shapes and sizes.

Some can even grow as BIG as this book!